Good Night,
Little Mouse

pictures by caroline anstey
story by dugald steer

templar publishing

It was time for Little Mouse
to go to bed and, after Grandpa
had read her a story, she wriggled
down under her snuggly quilt.
But no matter how she tossed and
tumbled or mumbled and grumbled,
she just couldn't get to sleep.
"Grandpa!" she called.
"I'm frightened!"

Grandpa came straight up to Little Mouse's
room to see what the matter was.
"I can't go to sleep, Grandpa!" said Little Mouse.
"It's dark and there are scary noises outside!"

"You needn't be afraid, Little Mouse!"
smiled Grandpa, giving her a cuddle. "The dark
can't hurt you! You are safe and snug in bed."
And with that, he went away again.

But just at that moment a gust of wind
must have blown outside for there came a loud
TAP TAP TAP
at the window. Little Mouse jumped.
"Grandpa!" she called.

Soon, Grandpa was at the door again.
"What's that tapping sound, Grandpa?"
asked Little Mouse.
So Grandpa took Little Mouse over
to the window, and showed her outside.
"Why!" said Little Mouse. "That tapping
sound was only the wind, blowing a
branch against the window!"

And just then, there was another sound.

It was a loud HOOT HOOT, far away.
Little Mouse looked very scared indeed!
"Don't you know what kind of bird hoots,
Little Mouse?" said Grandpa.

"Is it an owl?" asked Little Mouse.
"Yes!" exclaimed Grandpa. "Each night
Mother Owl leaves her nest to fly far
and wide over the countryside."
Just then there was another sound.

It was a BARK BARK BARK.
"I know that sound," cried
Little Mouse. "It's a dog!"
Noises didn't seem scary when
you knew what they were.

"No, Little Mouse,"
said Grandpa. "That isn't
a dog. Dogs sleep at night.
But foxes bark just like dogs.
Each night the fox leaves its den,
and sets off through the fields.
But you are safe, Little Mouse.
No foxes will come into the house."

"Let's listen and see if we can hear any other noises,"
said Little Mouse, and Grandpa agreed.
It didn't take long before
they heard a loud
SPLASH
from the stream
in the garden.

"Is that a bird?" said Little Mouse.
"Oh, no, Little Mouse," said Grandpa.
"Most birds sleep at night. That is an otter. Each night
he leaves his den, and dives into the stream for a swim."
Now, Little Mouse was starting to enjoy listening
for night sounds, but she did feel tired.
But she listened hard and heard a

patter patter patter

at the edge of the forest.
"Are they rabbits?" she asked,
giving out a big, sleepy yawn.

"Oh, no, Little Mouse,"
said Grandpa. "Rabbits curl up together
in their burrows at night. Those are another
night creature. They are badgers. If you
look hard you can see them, just at
the edge of the garden."

Little Mouse looked at the badgers,
then went back to bed. Now that she
knew what all the noises were she
didn't feel frightened any more.
"Thank you for coming to
see me, Grandpa!" she said.

Grandpa closed
the window and smiled.
"That's alright, Little Mouse," he said.
"I don't want you to be scared, so you will
always be safe and sound when I am close by."
But just as Grandpa leaned over to
hug Little Mouse and say, "Good night,"
what do you think he saw?